KLUNKY MONKEY

NEW KID IN CLASS

BY
ROBERT KRAUS

Silver Press

Library of Congress Cataloging-in-Publication Data

Kraus, Robert
    Klunky Monkey, new kid in class / by Robert Kraus.
       p.   cm. — (Miss Gator's schoolhouse)
    Summary: When new student Klunky Monkey's
constant sharing of his bananas makes all the animals in
school grow chunky like him, Miss Gator begins a shape-
up program for everyone.
    [1. Weight control—Fiction. 2. Monkeys—Fiction.
3. Animals—Fiction. 4. Schools—Fiction.] I. Title.
II. Series: Kraus, Robert, Miss Gator's schoolhouse.
PZ7.K868K1   1990
[E]—dc20   89-70199
    ISBN 0-671-70853-8 (lib. bdg.)   CIP
    ISBN 0-671-70854-6 (pbk.)   AC

Published by Silver Press, a division of
Silver Burdett Press, Inc.
Simon & Schuster, Inc.,
Prentice Hall Bldg., Englewood Cliffs, NJ 07632.
Printed in the United States of America.
10 9 8 7 6 5 4 3 2 1

Chapter 1
ALL ABOUT KLUNKY

Klunky Monkey was chunky.

He lived in a treehouse with his
mom and dad, Mr. and Mrs. Monkey.

They were chunky, too.

They sat in their treehouse
all day long, eating bananas.

They sat in their treehouse
all night long, eating bananas.

One day Klunky said,
"There must be more to life
than eating bananas.

I want to learn about the world.
I want to go to school."

So Klunky's mom gave him
a bunch of bananas
to take to school.
"In case you get hungry," she said.

And Klunky's dad flew him
to the little red schoolhouse
deep in the Hokey Smokey Swamp.

They were just in time.
Miss Gator was
ringing her bell,
and the other kids were
arriving.

First came Blake the Snake.

Then there was Ella the Bad Speller,

Punky Skunky, and Buggy Bear.

And right behind them

was Tardy Toad—

late as usual.

"Hi!" said Klunky.

"My name is Klunky."

"I'd say Chunky,"

hissed Blake the Snake.

Chapter 2
KLUNKY'S FIRST DAY

"Don't be rude, Blake,"
said Miss Gator.
"I'm sorry," said Blake.
"Have a banana,"
said Klunky.

Klunky passed out bananas

to all the kids in class.

16

"You already know one of the
first things we learn here,"
said Miss Gator.
"How to share."

But Klunky had a lot of
catching up to do in reading,
'riting, and 'rithmetic.

And the class had a lot of
catching up to do
in eating bananas.

So each day Miss Gator
and the class helped Klunky.
And each day Klunky brought
more and more bananas.

It was his way of saying

"Thank you."

Klunky learned more and more.

And the class became chunkier
and chunkier...

and chunkier...

and chunkier!

27

Then one day Buggy got stuck
in the door.

And when Ella sat down,
her desk broke.

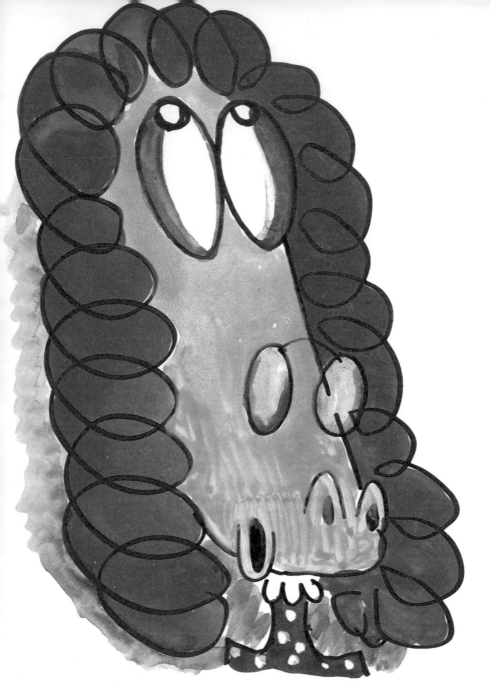

"This will never do,"
said Miss Gator.

Chapter 3
GETTING IN SHAPE

Bright and early
the next morning,
Miss Gator began
a shape-up program.

Miss Gator taught the class
how to eat the right foods.

"Bananas are okay," she said.

"But don't munch a whole bunch."

Miss Gator taught the class
how to exercise.

"Touch your toes with your
nose," she said.

"I can't see my toes,"
said Klunky Monkey.

"I don't have any toes,"
said Blake the Snake.

"If you move it, you'll improve it,"

Miss Gator told the class.

"Take a dive and look alive,"
said Miss Gator.

"If you bike it, you will like it,"
she said.

"And no thinking about bananas, Klunky."

"Row, row, row your boat,
gently through the swamp,"
Miss Gator sang.

"And no eating between meals."

Then Miss Gator led the class

in a jog around the swamp.

"Only eat when you're hungry,"
she said.

"I'm always hungry," said Klunky.

Soon the class looked like

their old selves again.

All except Klunky.

He looked better!